FLOWER KINGDOM SERIES™

JOHNNY

JOINS THE ARMY

BY ANDREA BEYERS

ILLUSTRATED BY ANTHONY ALEX LeTOURNEAU

Johnny Joins the Army
Flower Kingdom Series™
Copyright© 2008 by Andrea Beyers
Published by RockTuff Publishing

Scripture quotations used in the Flower Kingdom Series (TM) are taken from the HOLY BIBLE, NEW INTERNATIONAL
VERSION (R), Copyright(c) 1973, 1978, 1984 by the International Bible Society. Used by permission of Zondervan
Publishing House. All rights reserved.

The NIV version of the Bible is a translation which the author feels children can easily grasp. For that reason, it is
the version used as reference material in the Flower Kingdom Series(TM). The author, as well as the parties involved
in producing the Flower Kingdom Series(TM), would like it noted that its use therein is not an endorsement of, nor
condemnation of, any one translation, or version, of the Holy Bible over another translation, or version. If a parent,
guardian, or teacher would prefer to use a Bible translation, other than the NIV version, when reading, memorizing, and
sharing scripture with a child(ren); he or she should feel free to do so.

Cover Design by Anthony Alex LeTourneau
Illustrated by Anthony Alex LeTourneau
Layout and Design by Anthony Alex LeTourneau
Edited by Constance Buchanan

First Printing 2008
Printed in China
By Everbest Printing Co.
Through Four Colour Imports, Ltd.

ISBN 978-0-9800754-1-0

Library of Congress Control Number: 2008922359

ACKNOWLEDGMENTS

*Thank you Mom for tending that huge vegetable garden when I was a child. Thank you Linda for the many contributions you
wholeheartedly gave in the beginning. Thank you Connie for polishing the many rough edges of this story. Thank you Tony for
your sincerity, and your ability to do a job above anything I thought could be done. And, most importantly, thank you God for the
gift of salvation given through Jesus.*

-Andrea

PREFACE

Johnny Joins the Army is the second story in the Flower Kingdom Series. The fictional characters represent real children, adults, and animals, which live within plant and flower dwellings in the gardener's backyard. The gardener's backyard is comprised of the Flower Kingdom and the nearby Vegetable Village.

The Flower Kingdom kids, just like real children, are often confused and fearful when they encounter a problem. When Johnny Jump Up and Davy Dill presume they've been attacked, Davy's dad offers confusing advice. They then turn to a beloved animal for comfort. Deciding they know the answer on their own, they begin to wander from the truth.

Join them as they finally come to understand what it means to 'Join God's Army', realizing the value of forgiveness, and salvation, given through Jesus Christ's life, death, and resurrection.

Just for fun a sense of smell is highlighted throughout this story, as many of the homes within the fictional Kingdom and Village are quite aromatic! Head outdoors and discover for yourself the varied scents that nature has to offer. But first, turn the page and bury your nose inside the Kingdom…

My name is Johnny Jump Up. I live with my two aunts, Martha and Mary Pansy, in a Lily house. Most kids I meet want to know why I live with two Pansy aunts in a Lily. The fact is, we did use to live in a Pansy home, but it was only two rooms and we were always tripping over one another. One day Aunt Martha decided enough was enough, and being a savvy type, she snapped up a Lily house that had been on the market for two seasons. Much roomier! Aunt Martha said we bought the Lily for a song because not many home buyers could get past the color.

Our house *is* an ugly pink color, but it smells great. There is the fresh scent of the Lily petals, and Aunt Mary is always baking something sweet. Aunt Mary is the most famous cook in the entire Kingdom. And I am one of the luckiest kids. Because my bedroom is right next to the kitchen, I can sneak in before bedtime and grab a treat.

I hate to sit still, so most of the time I spend outdoors, jumping all over and exploring. Aunt Martha always makes a remark about me bringing half the Kingdom home on my shoes, they are so clogged with dirt. Aunt Martha is a bit picky. I have to waste a great deal of time cleaning my feet before being allowed inside…

This morning began like every other. Aunt Martha was worried about something.

"Mary, Johnny, come here. The roof looks awful!"

Aunt Martha mounted a stepladder and, standing on her tiptoes, inspected the petal roof. Then, with a sigh, she climbed back down and turned to me.

"Johnny, go to the Vegetable Village. A dose of compost to the roots of our Lily house will shine the roof right up again."

"But I want to play today!" I cried. Aunt Martha gave me one of her stern looks, lips pursed, as if she were sucking on a sour lemon. I knew what she was about to say:
God wants me to respect those in authority.

"Sorry," I piped up before she could utter the words. "I'll do it."

Aunt Martha smiled and handed me a bucket. "You better hurry up, there's the bus coming around the corner right now."

The huge gray-brown rabbit bus hopped toward the nearby stop. I jumped as quickly as I could, catching its tail just in the nick of time.

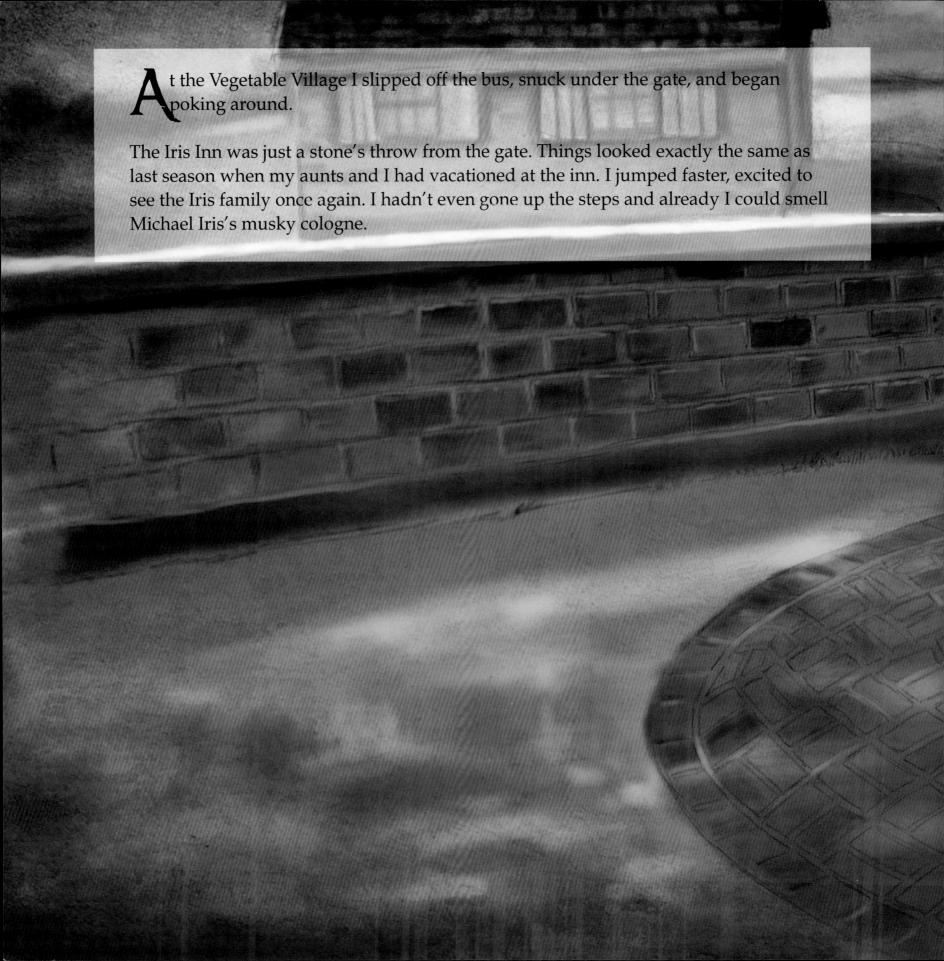

At the Vegetable Village I slipped off the bus, snuck under the gate, and began poking around.

The Iris Inn was just a stone's throw from the gate. Things looked exactly the same as last season when my aunts and I had vacationed at the inn. I jumped faster, excited to see the Iris family once again. I hadn't even gone up the steps and already I could smell Michael Iris's musky cologne.

"Well, if it isn't Johnny Jump Up!" Michael Iris boomed, answering my knock. He stepped onto the porch and swept me up in a giant bear hug. Embarrassed and overwhelmed by his cologne, I gasped for breath. "You sure have sprouted since last season," he said.

Even so, at over six inches tall, Michael towered over me. He looked every bit the aspiring owner of a busy inn. His purple-black hair was smoothed up and away from his face, his white shirt sparkled underneath his bright green vest and tie, and he wore a fitted green jacket with tails.

Michael eyed my bucket. "Let me guess—your Aunt Martha sent you for some compost?"

I laughed and nodded.

"Are you chatting with a visitor again?" a voice came from within.

"Be there in a minute, Carol!" Michael winked at me.

"Hurry up, sweetheart, I have another box to move."

"Who's that?" I said.

"That is Carol, queen of the Columbines. Remember her? I finally convinced her to marry me!"

"What made her change her mind?"

He chuckled. "Who can explain the workings of the heart? The Columbine queen is not the usual queen, thank goodness. She fell for a lowly innkeeper."

"I thought it was your parents who ran the inn."

"No, they're getting older, so I've pretty much taken over. I don't know if I could do it without Carol's help. What an angel! It's not like she doesn't have responsibilities of her own, too—she's in charge of the princesses at the Columbine castle. They're her nieces. In fact, today we're moving my things over there. Our plan is to work at the inn during the day and to spend our nights at the castle." Nodding toward the castle, which loomed above the inn, he moaned. "What an adjustment! My new nieces stay up and giggle half the night. And I have to wait forever to get into the bathroom. Living with so many princesses is driving me—"

"Michael," the voice cut in, "I'm going to throw out your ties if you don't come help me…"

"My ties!" Michael said with a start. "They aren't hurting anything."

"There are so many I can't fit them all in the box. I don't know any other man who hangs on to ratty-looking ties when he has so many brand new ones. You can't possibly wear all these!"

Michael glanced up at the sky and sighed loudly. Then he took off his coat, rolled up his shirtsleeves and loosened his tie. "Johnny, I have some business to take care of. Stop by on your way back, will you? It would be great to catch up."

I headed off to the compost hill, a huge pile the gardener had made with kitchen waste, grass clippings, and dead leaves. Gathering compost was not my favorite errand.

As I approached it, crinkling my nose at the sour smell of rotting organic matter, I heard someone singing. It was the voice of a boy, belting out a song about some guy named Ollie Lew. He sure knew how to hold a tune.

The singing grew louder, and soon the boy appeared. His green shirt was covered with yellow stripes. He had a brown face, large brown eyes, and curls that sprang from his head in all directions. For some reason, he was carrying a broken eggshell. As the boy walked closer, I noticed a familiar scent. Strange, I thought to myself, he smelled a bit like the pickles I put on my hamburger.

"Hello there!" he trilled. "I'm Davy Dill. What brings you to the Vegetable Village today?"

"I'm Johnny Jump Up, from the Flower Kingdom." I held up the bucket and crinkled my nose again. "I have to get some compost…"

Davy burst into song:

Oh, I will come along with you,

I love to slide, I really do.

Although the compost hill smells nasty,

Sliding down it makes me happy!

T hen he resumed his song about that Ollie Lew guy.

As we walked along, I noticed a tall dwelling covered with striking orange-red flowers. It was unlike any house or castle I had ever seen. "What's that?" I said, pointing.

Davy stopped singing. His smile vanished and a shudder ran down his spine. "That's where the Bean family lives," he whispered. "This is their first season in the Village. A few months ago, the gardener placed poles in the ground, and within no time, that Bean home grew to the top of the poles and formed a tent."

I gazed up at it, popeyed. "It's even taller than the Hollyhock castle in the Flower Kingdom!"

"Watch out, one of those Bean girls is trouble," Davy said in a low voice.

I wasn't sure what he meant. It sounded ominous. But he quickly shook off whatever was bothering him and belted out the refrain to his favorite song: "Ollie Lew, Ollie Lew, Olleee-Lewww-Ya!"

Then he dashed ahead to the compost pile. "Come on, let's slide down the hill before you fill that bucket!"

"No thanks," I said, following on his heels.

Davy scrambled up the hill with his eggshell, humming all the way to the top. To us Kingdom kids, a compost hill is as high as a mountain, and I had to crane my neck for a view of him. Afraid of heights, I wasn't about to go up there myself.

Davy found a flat spot and set the eggshell down. "I'll see you in a minute!" he yelled, hopping onto the shell. Then with a flick of his hands against the ground, he started sliding down the hill, springy locks of hair bouncing. He gathered speed as he descended, and all the while he was belting out his song about Ollie Lew.

"That bucket of yours would be perfect to store a bit of honey in…," a sweet voice whispered, catching me by surprise.

I whirled around and came face to face with a short girl wearing an orange-red dress and matching bandanna.

"Hello," she said, laughing at my slack-jawed expression. "My name's Scarlet Rosemary Bean. You can call me Scarlet for short. I live with my family in a tent over there. From my room at the very top I can reach over to a honeycomb. Right now it's dripping with honey."

I asked her what honey was.

"You've never tasted hon-ey?!"

"No…"

"Why, it's sweeter than the morning dew. Why don't you have a taste for yourself?" Motioning me to join her, she started scaling the wall of her tent.

I backed away, shaking my head.

"What's wrong?" Scarlet called down.

I looked down and kicked the dirt. "I'm afraid of heights," I mumbled.

"Afraid of heights, did you say? Why, that's silly." She came scooting back down. "Here, let me borrow your bucket. I'll bring you some back."

Without lifting my eyes, I handed her the bucket.

In a flash she was gone.

D avy came up, panting from his adventure. His hair was matted with scraps of kitchen waste–coffee grinds, cherry pits, and potato peels.

"Come on, Johnny, it's a blast!" He shoved the eggshell into my hands.

"Nah, I don't feel like it," I said, embarrassed to admit my fear of heights. "I'm just going to fetch some compost."

"In what?" he said, noticing my empty hands. "Your bucket's disappeared."

"Oh, a girl named Scarlet borrowed it to bring me some honey."

"Scarlet — Scarlet Rosemary Bean?" Davy groaned. "No — please tell me you didn't!" He circled around me, muttering, "You'll never see your bucket again…"

Never see it again? Aunt Martha would be furious!

"Come on, my dad will know what to do," Davy said, grabbing me by the arm.

The Dill home, several stories high, grew next to a brick wall which seperates the Kingdom from the Village. As we approached, a strangely familiar smell, a bit like pickles, hung thick in the air. My eyes began to water and I tried to hold in a sneeze.

"Ahhh-choo!" I rubbed my watering eyes, and wiped my nose, trying not to sneeze again.

"Bless you." Davy said. Then he sighed loudly and looked a bit embarrassed, "Johnny, I have to tell you something. Our home smells a bit funny. I think that is what is making you sneeze." Davy shrugged as I sneezed again and gasped for air.

"The smell is so strong it even sticks to my clothes and my hair, and nothing I do seems to get rid of it. I've grown used to it and don't really mind it. But, some people find being inside of our Dill home to be unbearable."

So that explained the smell of pickles when we first met, I thought to myself.

A man, whom I assumed to be Davy's dad, came from the entryway of the home.

Davy blurted out, "Dad, this is Johnny, Scarlet stole his bucket. I told you she's no good!"

"Hello, Johnny, Daniel Dill," the man said, holding out a hand. Davy's dad looked identical to Davy, only larger. Then he turned to his son. "Davy, I know how you feel about Scarlet, but—"

"We have to get it back," Davy said. He kicked a stump on the path's edge. "You always say we should be good soldiers. This is war!"

Davy's dad raised an eyebrow. "I don't know if you're old enough…"

"I'm almost the same age as David when he defeated Goliath. And you told me I was named after King David from the Bible."

"Okay then. But before starting a war you need to learn how to fight a battle."
He tapped his cheek. "Now, who knows a lot about soldiering?"

"You, Dad, you used to be a soldier!" Davy started jumping up and down, clapping his hands.

"Okay, let me tell you how to be a good soldier."

Davy took one last leap into the air, then landed cross-legged at his dad's feet and sank his chin in his hands, an intent look in his eyes. I settled down beside him.

"You need to spread the message as far as possible," Daniel said. He opened his arms to include the entire Village. "The best way to be a soldier is actually not to be like a soldier, but rather to be like a gardener! You need to plant seeds. Planting seeds isn't always easy though. Sometimes, in order to spread a seed somewhere new, we need to be willing to scale a tall brick wall." He pointed to the brick fence dividing the Village from the Kingdom.

"But Dad, we can't climb the brick wall—Johnny's afraid of heights," Davy said. I cringed with embarrassment, he'd guessed my secret.

"Well, spreading seeds is what I would do," Daniel said. It was clear from his tone that he wasn't going to entertain other options.

"But Dad—"

"Wait a minute," I said. "Whenever I am upset I talk to my friend Timothy. He always makes me feel better. I'd like to go visit him now."

"Who's that?" Davy said.

"Timothy is one of the tigers who roams around the lily trees near our home in the Flower Kingdom. Don't worry, he's tame and wouldn't hurt anyone." I quickly added. Davy's dad shook his head, muttering, "I don't know why you think you should waste time visiting an animal when you need to be spreading seeds…"

"Look, there's the bus!" I cried. "Come on, Davy, let's catch it."

"Mind you, Davy, be back before dinner," Daniel said.

Davy shoved the eggshell into his father's hands. "Hide my sled in the hall so no one steals it, will ya, Dad?"

Sighing, Daniel grabbed it, then promptly clicked his heels and dismissed us with a salute.

Back in the Kingdom, we snuck our way along the path. We needed to keep an eye out for my aunts. The last thing I wanted was for them to catch me back in the Kingdom, without a bucket of compost!

Timothy's huge striped body was nearly as large as the spindly lily trees around him. He perked up and leaned his head down to greet me. I stroked his ears, lovingly. Davy was aghast with fear. Timothy smiled eagerly at Davy.

"Timothy wouldn't hurt anyone!" I explained. Davy eyed Timothy with growing curiosity.

"Are you sure he's tame?" Davy asked.

I sighed. It always took a while for others to be convinced that Timothy was loyal and kind.

"Timothy, I don't know what to do! Someone stole Aunt Martha's bucket and I have no clue how to get it back. I am going to be in big trouble." I hung my head and Timothy put a paw on my shoulder. Then he stretched out on the ground, as he often does, inviting me to snuggle up and tell him the rest of the story.

"Oh, no, I can't lay around in the sunshine with you today. I have a serious problem to take care of!" He seemed to frown. Then he rose up on his back legs and closely examined Davy with narrowed eyes, his tail rising in the air behind his back.

"I am beginning to think my dad was right, Johnny, what good is it going to do talking to an animal?" Davy backed away from Timothy's gaze.

"Timothy is a great listener, aren't you?" I said, putting my hand under his giant chin. Timothy purred happily and nodded, tail swishing from side to side.

His head loomed above Davy's curls. He lowered his nose to Davy's t-shirt, sniffing curiously. His nostrils began to twitch. He began to moan…

Timothy shook his head and batted at his nose, as if to get rid of the lingering smell. Suddenly Timothy sneezed, unleashing a giant gust of air that flattened Davy's curls.

"That's it!" Davy announced. "I am telling my dad we need to find a house that doesn't leave a bad smell on my clothes!"

I began to laugh. "The smell is really not that bad. I kind of like it! Timothy just has a sensitive nose."

Davy turned to me. "We don't need to talk to anyone further, animal or adult, Johnny. Let's just go back to the Village and defeat Scarlet with our own two—"

Timothy put his paw on top of Davy's head, startling him speechless. Then his nose began to twitch again, gearing up for another giant sneeze. Davy's eyes grew round with worry.

"He's making a huge ruckus with his sneezing. Let's get out of here before your aunts catch us!"

Davy grabbed me and we headed back to the bus stop.

"Why're you so mad at Scarlet, Davy?" I said on the bus ride back to the Vegetable Village.

"Hmmpf!" Davy snorted. "That no-good thief! I didn't have any troubles at all until she moved to the Village."

He wouldn't tell me why, so I dropped the subject. Minutes later we slid off the bus by the Village gate and headed down the path past the Iris Inn.

Michael Iris, who had cast off his coat and changed his tie to a purple one, was sweeping the porch, humming the same tune that Davy had been humming all day. From inside the inn, a woman's voice was singing it too. This Ollie Lew fellow sure must be famous, I thought, to have so many people singing about him…

"I see you met each other, boys," Michael called to us as we passed by.

"We don't have time to talk right now, Michael. We're launching a counterattack," Davy announced. Stopping short, he snapped off a salute in Michael's direction and nudged me to do the same. (The salute I managed was not quite as crisp.) Then Davy clicked his heels together and pushed me forward on the path.

Michael set his broom aside. "Whoa, there!" he called after us. "I know some people who could help you with that."

D avy twirled around. "Oh yeah?"

"Yes, my parents. Come on in."

Reluctantly, we made our way toward the inn. Carol the Columbine queen was on the porch.

Michael bent to kiss her and the queen's pet ladybugs swooped down, grabbed hold of a piece of the side-swept, wrinkled hem of her gown, lifted it, and let the silky yellow material settle into place around her ankles.

Michael ducked inside the inn and the queen turned to us. Her pet ladybugs were circling Davy's hair, buzzing to each other about his strange scent. Davy swatted them away, annoyed, and Carol ordered them to retreat. They promptly settled down near her feet, chattering with each other.

"I remember meeting you last season, Johnny!" Carol cooed. She took my hands in hers, then spread my arms wide to gauge how much I had grown since she last saw me. I closed my eyes and breathed in her sweet scent.

"As for you, Davy, I can't stop singing that song you taught me — all my nieces in the castle join in with me." She began to hum Davy's tune as she slipped an arm around his shoulders.

"Who is this Ollie Lew?" I blurted out. "Everyone seems to know but me!"

The queen threw her head back and burst out laughing, nearly losing her crown.

Stifling a grin, Davy patted me on the back and said, "Johnny, alleluia isn't a person named Ollie Lew. It's a word that means 'praise God.'"

"Oh, that's priceless — funniest thing I've ever heard!" Carol gasped, shaking her head. "See you, boys, I have to go back to the castle." Still laughing, she waved goodbye and made her way down the steps, the ladybugs buzzing ahead of her.

"Ollie Lew," I could hear her saying to herself as she disappeared down the path, "priceless!"

U pset, I headed inside the inn with Davy. Michael's parents, James and Eloise Iris, were sitting on bulb chairs in the lobby. We plopped down at their feet.

"Michael tells us you boys want to launch a counter attack against someone," Eloise Iris said. She fluffed her hair. Though she was getting on in years, she still had lively blue eyes, and her stylish loose green pants and top took ten years off her age. She looked pointedly at Davy and continued, "The thing you need to ask yourselves is whether you've joined God's army, or just formed one of your own."

"God's army?" I echoed, confused.

"Yes," James Iris said with a smile. "Those who join God's army believe in Jesus Christ and are eager to spread His message of love."

Love? "You mean the people in God's army don't fight?" I said.

"They do wage battle, but it's not the kind you're thinking of."

"But soldiers go to war," Davy objected. "Johnny and I have been attacked!"

Eloise put her hand on Davy's shoulder. "When I say that we believers wage battle, I mean it in a spiritual sense. When we're attacked spiritually, we're at risk of losing our faith in God." She paused, considering her words. "As a general rule, Christian soldiers don't harm others. The battle is internal, and for the most part unseen."

"Oh," my friend said, his face falling. He sure did want a battle.

Eloise folded her hands in her lap. "Actually, we believers do have an enemy-Satan," She said. "While we are sinful by nature; Satan also tempts us to sin. Fellow believers can help other believers avoid temptations from our enemy. Believers can also remind everyone of the need to confess our sins and repent, or change, from a sinful way of life. Because God does not want believers to fall away from their faith, and because He wants the good news of salvation spread to all people, we often call the body of believer's God's army, and the individuals in that army, Jesus' followers, soldiers. We also often refer to the Bible as our sword or weapon. We don't mean this literally, just symbolically."

D avy looked as confused as I felt.

Seeing this, James waved me over and put an arm around my shoulder. "Johnny," he said, "tell us what Davy's dad taught you today."

"He taught us that the best way to be a soldier was to spread seeds as far as possible…," I began haltingly.

Eloise smiled. "See, Daniel was talking about being a symbolic soldier for God. It's important to spread God's love far and wide, to plant a seed in a new place and let it grow."

"What in the world is all this seed business?" Davy blurted. "What does that have to do with anything?"

"Davy, have you forgotten the message of salvation?" James asked.

"Of course not! Jesus Christ, God's one and only Son, came into the world, lived, died, and was resurrected, for the forgiveness of all of our sins."

At last it began to dawn on me, and I spoke up. "We are supposed to spread the message that we all have sinned, and we all can be forgiven, and given eternal life through belief in Christ. We can't make another believe, just like we can't make a seed grow in the ground. All we can do is share the story. Is that what everyone means by 'planting a seed'?"

"Yes!" James said. "We can't make someone believe, or give someone faith, but when we share the message of repentance and forgiveness through Christ, we figuratively plant a seed in a heart. Planting seeds, and spreading the message, is what we are called to do as God's soldiers! God does the rest, He makes that seed take hold in another's life and heart."

"It all starts with being friendly toward other people. Take an interest in what other people around you are doing. After a person considers you a friend and trusts you, you can easily share the good news of God's love." He paused. "There's just one little catch…"

"What?" Davy and I chimed.

"Jesus loved his enemies."

avy looked as if he'd just been stung by a bee. His face twisted up. His springy locks of hair trembled.

"Why, Davy Dill," Eloise exclaimed, "whatever on earth is wrong?"

"I'll never forgive Scarlet!" Davy blurted out. "When she moved to the Village, everyone insisted I play with her and make her feel at home. Well, I did my duty and taught her how to slide down the compost hill. And how did she thank me? She turned around and stole my eggshell sled! I found what was left of it, crushed at the bottom of the hill. And now she's stolen Johnny's bucket. She's a thief, and if somebody doesn't—"

Davy's rant was interrupted by a loud cough. I turned and saw Michael in the doorway, his face beet red. "Umm, Davy, I overheard your conversation there, and I have a confession to make…" He swallowed. "Last week I had an urge to go sledding, and I couldn't find any good eggshells in the compost hill. You weren't around for me to ask so I borrowed yours. I got going too fast and hit a watermelon rind and shattered your sled. I'm so sorry!"

"Why didn't you tell me?" Davy snapped.

"I've been so busy moving it slipped my mind—honest! I meant to help you find a new sled right away. Come on, let's go and look for one."

"Naw, that's okay," said Davy. "I finally found another one. My dad stashed it in the hall so no one would take it…"

"Well, let's go sledding then!" Michael said, clapping him on the back.

"Michael James Iris," his mother chided, "you're a married man now, far too old to be sliding down the compost hill. When will you ever grow up?"

"Oh, Ma," Michael said, bending over and pecking his mother on the cheek, "you're never too old to slide down the compost hill!" She pretended to be disgusted, stifling her smile.

Michael turned to us. "Boys, I want you to go to the Bean tent. Perhaps Scarlet's there with Johnny's bucket. If she did trick Johnny, forgive her and ask her to come sledding with us. That's exactly what Jesus would do."

Davy and I said goodbye and made our way back to the Bean tent.

My friend had a request. "If Scarlet doesn't come down, will you climb up to her room and get her?"

I wanted to ask Davy why he couldn't—after all, he wasn't afraid of heights. But he looked so chagrined. His face was all washed out, and his hair seemed to have lost some of its spring. "Sure, Davy," I replied. "A good soldier doesn't let fear hold him back…"

As it turned out, Scarlet wasn't in her room. She was sitting by the smelly compost hill with the bucket full of honey, hands sunk in her chin, looking awful lonely.

"Where were you?" she said, jumping up.

My face turned red.

"I thought you stole the bucket," Davy mumbled, averting his eyes. "We went off to plan an attack against you…"

Scarlet reeled backward, hand over her heart. "What?!"

"I'm sorry," Davy mumbled.

For a few moments Scarlet just stood there, trying to digest what Davy had said.

"Hey," Davy said in a perkier voice, "you want to go sledding with Michael and Carol? They're coming soon and they want you to join us."

A smile broke over Scarlet's face. "Sure! Look, I dug up a grapefruit peel while I was waiting for you two…" She disappeared behind the hill and quickly reappeared, dragging the largest grapefruit peel I had ever seen. "It'll fit all of us and it won't break like an eggshell!"

I caught a whiff of the Columbine queen's perfume, and soon Michael and Carol appeared. Between her perfume and his cologne, the hill's sour smell was pretty much overpowered.

"Last one up the hill's a rotten eggshell!" Michael sang out, snatching Scarlet's huge sled and tearing up the slope. When he reached the top he glanced down, waving his arm. "Come on, Queenie, come on, Beanie, hop on this sled with me and have some fun. Who cares about your clothes?"

Giggling, Carol grabbed Scarlet by the hand and they started up. "Come join us, guys," Scarlet called over her shoulder.

Davy glanced at me. "It's all right, I'm going to stay down here with Johnny."

"Oh, no you're not!" I said. "A good soldier doesn't let fear hold him back…"

Poised like a runner at the starting block, I took a deep breath, then sprang forward and clambered up the hill. At the top, I looked down and decided that heights weren't so bad after all. I wasn't even dizzy.

"Come on!" Michael said, beckoning us onto the sled with the rest of them.

Arms locked around each other's backs, we went tearing down the slope, past coffee grounds and cantaloupe rinds and shriveled banana peels, screaming with delight all the way down.

I was covered in grime, but there was no time to clean up. The bus was coming, the last one returning to the Flower Kingdom before dinner. I snatched up the bucket of honey and hopped on.
On the ride home, I worried that Aunt Martha would scold me for bringing home honey instead of compost. I glanced nervously at the setting sun. It was getting very late…

Then I cast my fears aside and started humming. Before long I was belting out Davy's song, and everyone on the bus turned to stare at me: "Allelu—allelu—allelu—uu—jah!" I knew without a doubt that my aunts would be pleased about one thing: I had joined God's army!

EXPLORE THE TRUTH

Did you notice in the story how Davy Dill went from praising God in one breath to complaining about Scarlet in the next? Do you ever thank God only to end up complaining about someone shortly thereafter? It seems silly to go from singing God's praises and being thankful to complaining about other people, doesn't it? Yet most of us are guilty of that very thing. We must remember that Grace, given through Jesus' life, death, and resurrection, is the most important gift we have. Therefore we have little to complain about. Even if others try to harm us or steal from us, we can gladly sing praises and give God thanks for the gift of salvation through Jesus. No one can steal that from us.

Davy Dill's dynamic personality was inspired by the biblical King David. David was not only a famous warrior and the beloved king of Israel, but also a talented musician and an ancestor of Christ. He wrote many well-known psalms, including Psalm 23. David proved his trust in God as a mere boy when he confronted wild animals that threatened his sheep, and later when he faced the giant Philistine, Goliath, who threatened Israel.

Being a Christian soldier starts by fully trusting in God, just as the shepherd boy David did when he faced the wild animals and fought Goliath. If we trust God, He will provide the tools we need for soldiering: His word, the Bible, is our weapon, and our fellow believers are His troops.

TREASURE THE TRUTH

Ephesians 6: 11 Put on the full armor of God so that you can take your stand against the devil's schemes.

Luke 6:35 But love your enemies, do good to them, and lend to them without expecting to get anything back. Then your reward will be great, and you will be sons of the Most High, because He is kind to the ungrateful and wicked.

Phaseolus coccineus

SCARLET RUNNER BEAN SEEDS

NET WT. 2.5OZ

ANNUAL

Go Outside and Play!

Scarlet runner bean seeds are large and colorful. They can be planted directly into the soil in late Spring. Extremely easy to establish in most climates, their vines will quickly grow to the top of a tall pole, or trellis.

To build a bean tent, place several tall poles in a large circle, forming a cozy space to play under (leave room for a doorway!). Plant runner bean seeds in the soil at the base of the poles. The seedlings should sprout within a week, and begin to climb the poles within a month of planting. After flowering, edible beans will set on the vines. Pick them, cook them, and eat them! Or, if you wish, allow some of the bean pods to grow very large, and dry right on the vine. You can then harvest the colorful seeds. They look very pretty stored in a clear glass jar or vase! The seeds you harvested can then be planted all over again the following Spring.

Fun Facts About Dill

Originating in Asia, dill plants were also widely grown in Europe. In fact, ancient Greeks and Romans crowned their heroes with wreaths made from dill and laurel. Dill was eventually brought from Europe to America with the early colonists. Thought to not only freshen breath, but to also keep a person alert, dill seeds were often given to adults, and children, to chew on during daylong sermons and church meetings. As a result, the seeds became known as meeting seeds.

Dill has long been known for its medicinal benefits. Years ago a mixture of dill oil and water was commonly used as a sedative for colicky babies.

Aromatic dill plants attract butterflies, as well as many beneficial insects to a garden. Extremely easy to grow, it should be no problem to get some dill plants started in your own backyard!

FLOWER KINGDOM SERIES

COMING NEXT TO THE FLOWER KINGDOM SERIES

AUDREY LEARNS TO TRUST

Through the eyes of Princess Audrey Hollyhock, readers will catch a glimpse of royal life: floating on the backs of fish in the castle moat, sleeping in a bedroom on a tall castle spire, and ordering special meals from the castle chef.

But royal life isn't all roses! While her sisters are quite at ease behaving like proper royalty, Audrey is decidedly different. She has trouble following picky rules and being graceful, which is the reason she has had to spend two miserable years in a daily etiquette class taught by the very proper Miss Diana Daisy. One morning, after Audrey nearly destroys the classroom with her klutzy moves, Miss Diana announces that in addition to etiquette classes, Audrey will be enrolled in ballet. Maybe ballet will teach her how to be graceful.

The first ballet class is a disaster. Believing there is an easier way to learn how to be a proper princess, Audrey sets out on a journey through the Kingdom to find the answer, bringing some friends along. She and her companions discover the importance of praying, not to fulfill our own wishes, but to discern God's plan for our lives. In the end, Audrey learns to trust that God made her just the way she is for a reason—and that just the way she is is the best way to be!